MW00874594

"This is a short yet very inspirational story. What makes it very meaningful to me is the fact that I have known one of the authors, Steve Sombrero, for over three decades, and he has always been a source of inspiration and has tremendous integrity. It's nice to know that this book was written by an individual that 'walks the talk.'"

**Paul Yonamine, Chairman Emeritus,
Central Pacific Bank**

"Steve and Candice Sombrero have crafted a thoughtful and heartfelt message of hope, faith, and perseverance, set against the backdrop of a world urgently in need of inspiration. Their gentle guidance and wisdom, artfully presented in this colorful and entertaining book, will share with our young people the words that will help them make the most of the opportunities and challenges before them and enable them to enjoy fulfilling, rewarding lives."

**Mufi Hannemann,
Former Mayor of Honolulu,
President & CEO, Hawai'i
Lodging & Tourism Association**

"I absolutely love how Steve and Candice highlight the importance of present focus and the true meaning of living Aloha."

Rusty Komori, Author of *Beyond The Lines & Beyond The Game*

"*What Day Are You?* is a simple yet profound approach to successful living. A heartwarming story for people of all ages."

Scott Hogle, Bestselling author of *Divine Intelligence*

"*What Day Are You?* can be a cryptic question until you do the math. Then, it becomes a defining moment when the lights turn on. Steve and Candice, a father-daughter duo, offer children and adults alike the creative discovery of a successful life."

Dr. Wayne Cordeiro, Pastor/Author

"Storytelling has been a deeply rooted part of our island culture. It's how our Polynesian ancestors passed on important traditions and values. Steve Sombrero and Candace Ishikawa have woven together an enjoyable story that illustrates the importance of making the most of every day. Congratulations on this very entertaining book."

Kenneth Silva, Honolulu Fire Department Fire Chief, (ret)

"An epic story for all ages! I strongly believe that a little more Aloha: love, kindness, compassion, respect, and patience, with yourself and others, can go a long way. *What Day Are You?* beautifully captures the importance of living in the moment and embracing the Aloha Spirit."

Carissa Moore, Moore Aloha Foundation Founder, 5x World Champion Surfer & Olympic Gold Medalist, and Oahu native

"Navigating life, hardship, struggle, pressure, expectations, and anxiety isn't easy. *What Day Are You?* shares a simple yet profound message for staying present and embracing the Aloha Spirit. An empowering read for all ages!"

Yoshio Nakamura, Japan Ambassador to the Vatican, The Holy See

"Steve and Candice tell a beautiful and clever story about the power of our perspective. *What Day Are You?* highlights the importance of focusing on today, rather than emphasizing past experiences or future worries. This story also shows how to exercise grace and Aloha when interacting with others who may not be living in 'today mode.' These are valuable practices for people of any age."

Kristen H. Walter, Ph.D., Clinical and Research Psychologist

"*What Day Are You?* is a must-read for any teen who feels overwhelmed by the past or the future. It's a clever reminder that we should make today the most important part of our daily lives. Aloha."
Justin Speegle, Colonel, US Air Force (ret), Adaptive Surfing Instructor

A fool-proof blueprint for living a happier, more fulfilled life by embracing TODAY and savoring life's precious moments. Cherish the present; it's where happiness truly resides."
Kris Primacio, CEO of the International Surf Therapy Organization

"What Day Are You?"

"What Day Are You?"

A simple equation
for living life in the moment

By Steve Sombrero
& Candice Sombrero Ishikawa

Introduction

Laniakea Beach, also known as Turtle Beach, graces the world-famous North Shore of Oahu, Hawaii. A popular stop for visitors, it offers the chance to spot the green sea turtles basking in the sand, and if you're fortunate, even catch a glimpse of monk seals sun-bathing nearby. Laniakea comes from the Hawaiian term "Open Sky" and is nestled within a 7-mile stretch of pristine white sandy beaches. Its breathtaking beauty has earned a reputation as one of Oahu's most magnificent coastal treasures.

To the right of the beach, a rocky cove is sheltered by lush vegetation and swaying palm trees. Explore this haven, and you will encounter an array of delightful creatures such as hermit crabs, sand crabs, and vibrant tropical fish thriving in the tidepools.

ea
ach

ALOHA FROM THE ISLAND
- OF -

Oahu

tion

Kailua

makapu'u
Point

Diamond
Head

lu

While seated on Laniakea Beach, gentle trade winds caress your cheeks with a sweet and refreshing coolness. Time seemingly stands still, allowing you to absorb the beauty and energy of the ocean. Beyond the reef lies the vast expanse of the North Pacific Ocean, stretching for 3,000 miles until it meets the distant shores of Alaska.

What Day Are You is a fictional tale centered around the sea creatures inhabiting Laniakea Beach, featuring a young sea turtle who learns valuable life lessons from a wise, old hermit crab.

The phrase, "What Day Are You" not only asks a question but also presents a philosophy that encourages making today the most important part of your daily life.

The Lifeline:

Yesterday + Today = Tomorrow

It's a peaceful morning at Turtle Beach on the North Shore of Hawaii. The powdery beige sand stretches across algae-covered rocks, resembling a warm blanket draping over the rocky shoreline. To the east, sunlight sparkles on palm leaves that dance in the cool Pacific trade winds. It feels as though nature itself is listening to the music playing on this world-famous beach.

The waves at Turtle Beach are gentle and inviting, attracting a variety of sea creatures. Colorful tropical fish swim in schools, while monk seals go about their business undisturbed. Crabs emerge from their hiding places under the full moon, adding to the diverse array of marine life. Many sea creatures – too many to name.

Some prefer privacy, scurrying between rocks or burrowing into the sand, creating personal bubbles that no one dares to break.

Others love company—and they are not bothered by curious humans, either! These marine animals bask in the sand, unfazed, as two-legged creatures stroll along the beach very carefully so as not to disturb the sea creatures while marveling at the vast ocean.

MoCo is one such animal who thrives in being in the company of other species.

A curious and adventurous sea turtle, she spends her days drifting in the ocean or napping along the shoreline. Her youthful shell is smaller and shinier than other sea turtles who have lived in the neighborhood for nearly one hundred years.

MoCo faithfully follows her daily routine. Each morning, she leisurely feasts on a healthy breakfast of fresh sea grass.

Then she gracefully glides across the bay to visit her dear friend JiJi, a wise and elderly hermit crab who lives on the northwest end of Turtle Beach.

MoCo cherishes her daily visits with JiJi.

Not only is her senior buddy hilarious and entertaining, but he amuses her with stories about every creature in the neighborhood.

In fact, JiJi's nickname is "Mayor of Turtle Beach."

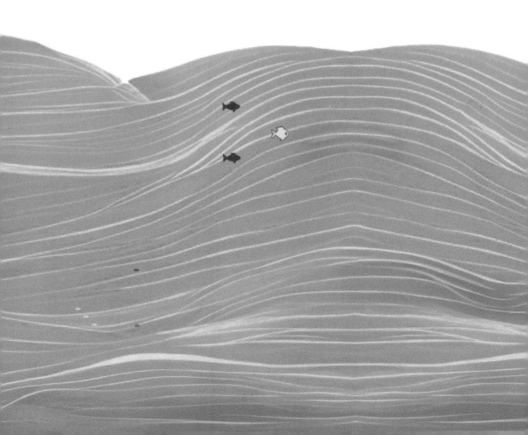

On this particular morning, as MoCo swims across the bay to see JiJi, she notices a school of tropical fish darting beneath her, swiftly maneuvering in and out of coral beds. Their vibrant, rainbow-colored parade inspires MoCo to join their dance routine! With her head tilted and fins swishing left to right, Moco sways to their synchronized beat, creating swirly clouds of sand that drive nearby residents to peer out of their private, rocky homes.

One of those residents is Uku—a mud crab with a notoriously grumpy disposition.

Spikes protrude from Uku's muddy-brown shell, and his massive pinchers look like weapons. Shaped like a heavy, dark anchor that sunk to the ocean floor centuries ago, Uku rarely strays from the muddy giant rock that he calls home.

On this particular morning, however, Uku hears laughter, so he decides to investigate.

Cautiously, taking one crabby step at a time,
Uku emerges from his hiding place and
spots MoCo and her fish companions
in the shallow water,
playing and squealing
with delight at their
newfound friendship.

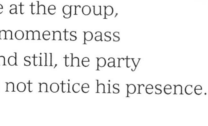

They're having
so much fun that
they don't notice
the mud crab.

Uku's dark eyes
glare at the group,
and moments pass
by and still, the party
does not notice his presence.

23

In outrage, Uku releases a long, angry grunt—blaring as loud as the tour helicopters that occasionally soar above Turtle Beach.

That finally catches their attention! Like a game of freeze tag, MoCo and the fish abruptly stop playing.

Another furious grunt escapes Uku's mouth, this time in short, staccato bursts.

Fearful, the tropical fish assemble like obedient soldiers and swiftly swim toward Turtle Beach in the southeast direction. MoCo lowers her head, as if to say "I'm sorry" to Uku and raises her right fin to wave "bye-bye" to her departing fish friends, secretly hoping for another opportunity to play together in the future.

Satisfied that he broke up the party, Uku retreats to his colossal rock.

Embarrassed, MoCo hastily swims out of Uku's territory. On her solo journey across the bay to visit JiJi, she feels shaken, alone, and scared.

The first thing MoCo sees when she arrives at JiJi's home is his elderly face and arms protruding out of an aluminum can. His bottom is inside the can, tightly wedged.

JiJi does not hear MoCo arrive. The hermit crab's eyes are closed, and his pinchers press together as if in deep thought or meditation.

MoCo hesitates, then calls out, "Good morning, JiJi!"

Startled by the sudden greeting, JiJi's tiny glasses slide off his face and begin to drift in the shallow water. He grabs the glasses before they float into the sea.

"Oh, good morning, MoCo!" says JiJi cheerfully, resting his glasses on top of his wrinkled forehead. "How are you today?"

"I'm very well, thank you! I brought you a small gift," MoCo opens her mouth and releases a clump of seaweed she gathered earlier during breakfast. The tuft of seaweed floats in the water toward JiJi, who is happy to accept the token.

"I like your new apartment!" MoCo giggles, tapping JiJi's aluminum can, which is much cleaner than his previous dwelling—a vintage, tuna can covered in rust and grime.

"Why, thank you, MoCo," JiJi chuckles. "It was time for an upgrade. This is my new retirement home."

MoCo's joyful face turns solemn. "JiJi, this morning, I passed by Uku the mud crab. What do you know about him? What's his story?"

JiJi breaks into a knowing smile, the aluminum can wiggling up and down as he nods at the young sea turtle. "Ahh, MoCo! I was hoping you would ask that question one day," JiJi says gently.

The hermit crab positions his glasses over his cataract-filled eyes and studies the young sea turtle.

MoCo smiles wide in anticipation.

"I cannot tell you anything about Uku yet," he says, with a serious tone. "He has lived in the neighborhood for a very, very long time."

"Why can't you tell me about Uku?" MoCo asks, pointing her head in the direction of Uku's home near the muddy rocks.

JiJi says, "First, you need to learn the Secret of the Lifeline. This is an ancient riddle that rules our ocean."

"The Lifeline?" MoCo asks, tilting her head.

"Yes. And when you understand the Lifeline, I am confident you will understand Uku—and other creatures of our ocean community."

MoCo, her youthful eyes full of curiosity, gazes at the elderly hermit crab, fascinated by his words. For the first time, she notices nicks on her friend's face, inflicted by ocean and sky predators during his lifetime.

JiJi—aluminum can attached to his bottom— slowly shuffles toward a patch of sand. It is bare and flat, untouched by rocks and seaweed. The hermit crab extends his right pincher to draw a straight, long horizontal line on the sand floor.

"This is the Lifeline," JiJi explains. "Imagine our lives flowing from one end to the other end. Time, you see, keeps slipping into the future."

He stands in the center of the line and points his left claw at the left tip of the line. "This end of the Lifeline is what we call, 'YESTERDAY.' And the opposite end," says JiJi pointing, "is 'TOMORROW.'"

MoCo nods her head and slowly shuffles around JiJi. "Perhaps you can complete the puzzle for me," prompts the hermit crab. "If YESTERDAY is here, and TOMORROW is there, the middle of the line where I am standing is called …"

"Today?" MoCo shrugs.

"Exactly!" says JiJi. "You are a bright, young turtle." MoCo beams. JiJi writes five big letters in the center of the line, "TODAY."

"Remember," continues JiJi, "the Lifeline comes with an important rule: Every day, the sun rises and the sun sets and we move from TODAY to TOMORROW. At the same time, what was TODAY becomes YESTERDAY."

MoCo nods, following JiJi's explanation.

The hermit crab continues, "In the Lifeline, the three elements interconnect: YESTERDAY, TODAY and TOMORROW. Every day, we pass through the elements. And this relationship is expressed in a mathematical equation: Yesterday + Today = Tomorrow."

To emphasize his point, JiJi walks the line, aluminum can apartment dragging along the sandy floor and exclaims, "Yesterday plus Today equals Tomorrow!"

MoCo squints and reads the equation in the sand, "YESTERDAY plus TODAY equals TOMORROW?

Wowee! I know math!" MoCo sings.

"You sure do!" JiJi says. "In fact, many of
the world's secrets and observations can be
expressed through mathematical equations.
In this math equation, the things that happen
YESTERDAY plus the things that happen
TODAY, determine what your TOMORROW
will be like."

With a smirk on her face, MoCo says, "So, like,
if I stay awake all day yesterday and today—
without taking naps—I will be tired tomorrow.
Then when tomorrow comes, I ..."

JiJi interrupts MoCo and chuckles, "You're
on the right track, MoCo.

"Wowee!" MoCo pipes. "I don't think of my life as a 'Line.' Now, I see why you call this the 'Lifeline.'" MoCo claps her fins. "What else, JiJi? Tell me more secrets!"

JiJi chuckles. "MoCo, I am very pleased that you understand the Lifeline. However, this is all I can teach you for now. It is getting late and young turtles need their afternoon naps. Besides, the next van of tourists will arrive at Turtle Beach very soon. I do not want you to miss the excitement."

MoCo nods obediently at her elder. "Alright, then goodbye, and thank you, JiJi!" she says, waving her fins and turning toward the shoreline.

JiJi yawns. Elderly hermit crabs need naps, too!

As she quickly swims across the bay, MoCo makes sure not to disturb Uku the mud crab. Like a submarine on a stealth mission, she swims past the grouchy crab's home navigating the tangled seaweed and muddy rocks.

No eye contact. No friendly greeting, nothing. Uku prefers it that way.

* * *

Uku carries a big secret. Little does MoCo know that Uku, hidden within the depths of his sanctuary, secretly listens to her daily conversations with JiJi. Across the water, their voices travel and reach the murky depths, where Uku eagerly listens. Eavesdropping is the highlight of Uku's life.

Above Turtle Beach, the midday sun shines directly overhead and beams downward like a thick, golden laser over the Pacific Ocean. Palm trees sway gracefully in the wind, and nature plays its music once again.

MoCo swims toward the reef where the water is cooler. As she bobs her head and paddles with her fins, she spots a bright orange van pulling into the parking lot.

The midday tour has arrived! A dozen tourists pour out of the vehicle and dash across the marked crosswalk toward Turtle Beach. Their chorus of voices grows louder, although MoCo has no clue about what they're saying, she senses their enthusiasm and it fills her with joy.

Overjoyed to welcome these two-legged creatures to the North Shore, MoCo races towards the rocky shore to bask in the sun on the sandy beach.

As the afternoon progresses and tourists snap pictures of a napping MoCo, JiJi's lesson travels across the bay, filling MoCo's dreams. The words of the lesson echo in her mind: "Lifeline. Yesterday Plus Today Equals Tomorrow."

66

Imagine our lives flowing from
one end to the other...

Time, you see, keeps
slipping into the future

Yesterday Mode

After waving "hello!" to two-legged
creatures all afternoon and sleeping
overnight on Turtle Beach, MoCo wakes
up next to algae-covered rocks near the
shoreline. Sparkly dry sand covers her wet
fins and belly like sugar-dusted malasadas.

It is early morning, and she isn't the only turtle in the area. Elderly sea turtles, who like to wake up before dawn, are eating breakfast together in the ocean. MoCo joins them, keeping a respectful distance so the senior turtles can search for food too.

Turtles are built for camouflage—it's tricky to spot dark-green sea turtles floating in the deep-blue water!

MoCo wants to visit JiJi again today, so she quickly fills her belly with sea grass and paddles toward JiJi's home on the northwest end of the bay. Sunlight beams through feathery clouds, creating warm pockets on the massive Pacific Ocean. The long, solo journey gives MoCo plenty of time to think about Uku the mud crab.

What is his story? Why did he break up yesterday's tropical-fish dance party? Why is he so angry?

MoCo's young brain craves answers. Warm water fills her nostrils, and a gentle current pushes her closer to where JiJi and Uku live. Suddenly, MoCo has an epiphany: "I know! Maybe Uku does not have friends! Maybe he just needs a buddy!". The young turtle, super excited by her revelation, paddles in the direction of Uku's home.

As she enters Uku's territory, MoCo spots the mud crab's piercing dark eyes staring at her. Half of his body is hidden by a rock. Still, MoCo enthusiastically swims toward him.

Taking a big deep breath, MoCo chatters, "Hi! My name is MoCo! I live at Turtle Beach. I know your name is Uku. Can we be friends?!"

The mud crab shakes his dark, stony head in disbelief as he crawls toward MoCo with a piercing glare. Pointing a dark claw at her like a medieval sword, he says, "I knew it! I knew you would return! Get out and stay out!" Uku's furious dark eyes shoot daggers at the startled young turtle, as he retreats behind the jagged rock—his safe space.

"Ohhh!" MoCo stutters. "I am very sorry, Uku! VEERYY, very sorry! I did not mean to disturb you."

Uku grunts and buries himself under the dried, brown leaves and thick mud. He wants the little sea turtle to leave him alone.

Stunned, MoCo quickly spins around and paddles in the direction of JiJi's neighborhood. Warm shame flushes her cheeks, and her little heart pounds like a toy drum.

What did she do to make Uku so angry? She genuinely wanted to be his friend.

When MoCo spots JiJi's shiny aluminum can in the distance, she quietly approaches, careful not to startle him like she did yesterday.

"Hiiiii, JiJi," says MoCo, almost in a whisper. Her fins droop beneath her shoulders, and her round head tucks into her shell.

"Hello MoCo!" says the hermit crab cheerfully, then notices the turtle's slumped demeanor, "Is everything alright?"

"Not really," MoCo admits, her tiny voice echoing from deep within her shell. "I made Uku mad this morning.

All I did was invite him to be my friend. But he yelled at me and said to leave and never come back. I don't understand what happened!"

"I see that Uku's reaction bothers you," JiJi replies. MoCo's head pops out of her shell, and she nods, relieved that another sea creature understands her.

"You do!?" she asks incredulously.

"Absolutely, it is normal to feel uncomfortable when another creature is upset at us," he reassures the young turtle. MoCo puffs her cheeks out, letting out a sigh.

"Do you remember the Lifeline I taught you yesterday?" JiJi asks.

"I do! Every day, the sun rises and the sun sets, and we move from TODAY to TOMORROW. At the same time, TODAY becomes YESTERDAY. And Yesterday plus Today equals Tomorrow." JiJi nods, pleased that she remembers.

"But what does Uku have to do with the Lifeline? I don't get it," MoCo says, shrugging her fins.

"Perhaps you will understand when I explain Rule #2 of the Lifeline," JiJi says, an all-knowing smile on his face. "With Rule #2, if you move any part of the equation to the other side of the equation, it becomes NEGATIVE." MoCo watches JiJi scrawl more symbols and words on the sand.

"This is what happens when we move TODAY to the other side of the equation, to the right side, to be exact. When we do that, TODAY becomes NEGATIVE. And the new negative equation looks like this:"

Yesterday = Tomorrow – Today

MoCo reads slowly, "YESTERDAY *equals* TOMORROW *minus* TODAY?"
"Ummm, JiJi? I still don't get it."

"You will in a second," JiJi assures her. "This new math equation is called YESTERDAY MODE meaning that YESTERDAY is now front and center of the Lifeline.

And because TODAY is now negative, the only thing left on the other side of the equation is Tomorrow. For this reason, the things that happened YESTERDAY will repeat TOMORROW unaffected by what you do TODAY."

"Ohhh, I see," MoCo says. "Yesterday Mode! But what does this have to do with Uku?"

"Uku *is* this equation, you see. Uku lives in Yesterday Mode," Says JiJi.

MoCo shakes her head, utterly confused. JiJi continues, "Yesterday Mode is a thought process that follows a certain, predictable pattern:

1. Today does not matter, because it is a negative.
2. Tomorrow mirrors Yesterday, so you expect tomorrow to be just like Yesterday.

3. The things that happened Yesterday, are
   what matter the most."

JiJi continues, "It can be easy for anyone
to fall into this thought pattern and believe
that negative things from YESTERDAY
will repeat themselves TODAY. Then when
TOMORROW comes—and TOMORROW
always comes—it becomes difficult to stay
positive, no matter how happy TODAY
might be."

MoCo's eyes widen. "Is Uku worried that
yesterday's events might happen again,
today?"

JiJi pinches tiny grains of sand off his
whiskers. "Correct. And that's why he yelled
at you to leave and never come back."

"I see!" MoCo says, now understanding the new mathematical equation. "It's like a wave. Sometimes, when a huge wave pushes me into the ocean, I get scared that another wave will come back and push me again and flip me upside down. But that doesn't stop me from going back to the ocean the next day!" MoCo wrinkles her nose. "Ugh, I don't wanna be stuck in Yesterday Mode."

"Me too," JiJi nods, holding up a claw. "Yesterday Mode is like my squeaky old pinchers here. When I hold onto something too tight, it's hard for me to let go. Every day, I do my best to let go—and not be stuck in Yesterday Mode."

MoCo tilts her head to the left. "So, JiJi, what happens when we get stuck in this mode? This Yesterday Mode?"

JiJi isn't quite sure how to answer MoCo's earnest question. The elderly hermit crab looks down at the sand, contemplating the math equation he had just written. He presses his claws together, closes his eyes and takes long, deep breaths.

MoCo watches, patiently waiting for the hermit crab to answer. Sometimes, JiJi takes a long, long time to reply to her questions. So, she studies the math scrawled on the sand, memorizing its important message.

Yesterday = Tomorrow – Today

When MoCo looks up, she is shocked to see tears in JiJi's eyes. The hermit crab removes his foggy glasses and shakes off the sorrow. Tears splash onto the sand like tiny raindrops.

JiJi says slowly, "What happens, MoCo, is that our hopes and dreams fade. And if we repeat Yesterday Mode, every day on the Lifeline, we begin to disappear, too. Sometimes, forever."

MoCo's eyes widen again. "Ohhhhh," she breathes, sadly.

* * *

Behind his giant rock, Uku sinks lower into the wet mud and bed of dry leaves. His weight is an anchor, his body listless as he eavesdrops on the turtle and hermit crab.

Tears flow from Uku's dark eyes too.

*When you hold on to something
too tight, it's hard to let go…*

Every day, do your best to let go...

Tomorrow Mode

More than half a day passes, and MoCo loses track of time as the morning sun crawls over the bay and travels west. After a long conversation about Uku and YESTERDAY MODE, JiJi wants to lift MoCo's spirits, so he entertains the laughing turtle all afternoon with lively stories about neighborhood sea creatures.

He tells her about the mama whale who visits from Alaska during the holidays— with an adorable new baby every other season. And the star fish, who claims to be able to point to true North no matter where he is on the beach because he believes his arms are magnetized.

"More stories! Tell me more, please, JiJi?" MoCo begs, after JiJi finishes a tale.

JiJi wants to oblige, but it is getting late. As the sun dips into the horizon, the hermit crab offers to accompany her on the long journey back to Turtle Beach.

"Sure! Climb onto my shell," MoCo
cheerfully says. "I will swim us home and
introduce you to my neighborhood in the
morning. The turtles won't mind if you
stay overnight."

JiJi climbs onto MoCo's shell, and she
paddles home. The moon is full and orange,
casting an ethereal glow across the bay. JiJi
carries his glasses so that they do not fall
into the ocean. He can barely see the palm
trees dancing hula with the ocean breeze.
Further in the distance, blurry headlights
illuminate the highway next to Turtle Beach.
Because his vision isn't so great, JiJi shuts
his eyes and inhales the salty sea air, listens
to the waves, and feels the cool breeze swirl
around him and MoCo.

MoCo and JiJi safely reach the sandy shores of Turtle Beach, where elderly sea turtles are already sleeping on algae-covered rocks. Their snores are a seaside symphony—but much louder than the cymbal of waves crashing on the shore.

MoCo finds a large, flat rock on which she can rest—with JiJi on top of her shell. As she gazes at the full, bright moon, she inhales the scent of the salty ocean, and her breathing syncs with the rhythm of the waves. Sleepiness comes over her.

Suddenly, a tiny movement below their rock startles the duo. MoCo glances over her shoulder at JiJi, and the elderly hermit crab adjusts his glasses to inspect the sand. MoCo looks up at her friend, "What's that, JiJi?"

Another tiny movement causes the sand to wiggle. JiJi peers through his glasses. "Do you see that?" the hermit crab whispers. "I think that's my old pal WiKi the ghost crab!"

Sure enough, a lone ghost crab squeezes his body into a deep hole, then quickly climbs out and scurries across the sand. His pale body is almost translucent under the full moon. Using his tiny pinchers like a mini shovel, the ghost crab ferociously digs another hole until the dark abyss is deep enough for him to enter.

JiJi puts a claw to his mouth as if to stifle a laugh. He and MoCo both stare at the hole, wondering what the ghost crab would do next.

The pale, little creature climbs into the hole—and disappears. A few seconds later, he emerges out of the hole and plunges his pinchers into the sand again to frantically dig another hole. Like a playlist on repeat: Dig hole, enter hole, climb out of hole; dig another hole, enter hole, climb out of hole. MoCo and JiJi look at each other, clearly amused.

"That is WiKi!" JiJi whispers.

The ghost crab has a name! Excited to make a new friend, MoCo loudly whispers, "Hello! Are you WiKi? My name is MoCo. It's nice to meet you!"

The ghost crab raises his pincher mid-air and startles at the child-like voice. His white face looks up to see MoCo and JiJi, staring down at him from their flat rock. WiKi recognizes JiJi and salutes.

In a hoarse voice, the ghost crab responds, "Aloha! Mayor!" The two-worded reunion is complete. Not missing a beat, WiKi returns to work, his little body scurrying across the sand to dig another hole.

MoCo observes, "Your friend sure looks like he's in a hurry. Why's he digging so many holes?"

MoCo looks at JiJi seeking an explanation. Instead of answering, the hermit crab climbs down from her friend's shell, jumps onto the sand and begins carving words into the algae.

Though MoCo can only see his aluminum can. In the moonlight, she notices the words 'ALOHA' imprinted on the can.

JiJi turns to face MoCo and points at the writing:

$$-\text{Tomorrow} = -\text{Today} - \text{Yesterday}$$

MoCo says, "This looks like more math. 'Negative TOMORROW equals negative TODAY minus YESTERDAY?' Why are there a lot of negatives?"

"You'll understand in a minute," JiJi says, smiling at the earnest turtle. "Seeing my old pal WiKi inspires me to teach you another lesson about the Lifeline."

JiJi points at the algae. "In this new math equation, we move TOMORROW to the other side of the equation, to the left side, to be exact. And we move Yesterday and Today to the right side of the equation. When we do that, TOMORROW becomes NEGATIVE. This causes everything on the right side of the equation, TODAY and YESTERDAY, to also become negative."

"I get it. But what does this have to do with WiKi?" MoCo asks.

"Remember what I taught you about YESTERDAY MODE?" JiJi asks. "This new mathematical equation describes what's called the NEGATIVE TOMORROW MODE."

JiJi continues, "NEGATIVE TOMORROW MODE is a thought process that follows when you bring TOMORROW front and center of the equation. A predictable pattern begins to take place, like this:

1. Tomorrow is all that matters and it has become negative.
2. Yesterday does not matter because it is also negative.
3. Today also does not count because it is also negative."

MoCo nods. "So, WiKi is stuck in NEGATIVE TOMORROW MODE?"

JiJi replies, "Correct. WiKi once told me— years ago—that he keeps on moving because pausing makes him uncomfortable and anxious about the future. And because of his anxiety, WiKi is never satisfied with the holes that he digs, worried that they are either too small or too big, too close to the ocean or too far away.

Instead, he is obsessed, eternally digging and searching for that one perfect hole. I do wish WiKi made the choice to rest and enjoy the evening with us."

MoCo bobs her head in agreement as she gazes at the moon over Turtle Beach with its lights shimmering across the bay.

"Ugh, I don't wanna be in Negative Tomorrow Mode, at least not *all* the time," she says. "I want to pay attention to today and remember the good things that happened yesterday."

MoCo's eyes scan the sand for the ghost crab, WiKi. She wants to invite him to notice the full moon, feel the ocean breeze, experience camaraderie, and be her friend. However, WiKi is nowhere in sight. Perhaps he is inside a newly dug hole, inspecting his craftsmanship.

MoCo turns to the hermit crab, "JiJi,
what happens when we get stuck
in Negative Tomorrow Mode?"

JiJi nods but instead of speaking, he points
his right claw toward the ocean, where
the tide is beginning to rise. Under the
moonlight, MoCo and JiJi notice WiKi
running back and forth, surrounded by more
freshly dug holes – nearly twenty of them.
It's a masterpiece! The ghost crab surveys
his work for a few seconds then plunges
a claw into the sand, frantically digging
another hole.

"I do admire that WiKi lives with a sense of
purpose," JiJi says, watching the ongoing
construction.

Bored of watching the ghost crab on repeat, MoCo turns her head toward the ocean to enjoy the scenery. Suddenly, she gasps! A loud roar fills the air like an angry motor, as a gigantic wave rolls in WiKi's direction. It grows larger and more ferocious, racing toward the shoreline as if sprinting for a gold medal.

MoCo yells, "WiKi! WATCH OUT!" But her teeny voice is overpowered by the roaring wave.

It's too late. The barreling wave charges at WiKi, who remains oblivious inside his hole. WHAAAAOOOOOSH!! The almighty wave engulfs WiKi and his holey kingdom. As the wave retreats to the ocean, WiKi emerges from the wet, flat sand, his crabby body dripping with saltwater. "Ohhhhh, WiKi," MoCo mourns.

Stunned, the ghost crab's round eyes survey
the damage caused by the monster wave.
He zigzags left and right across the sand,
tripping over his own legs and flailing
his claws in the air. Panicking, WiKi races
inland, away from the shoreline, to conquer
another section of sand - a perfect spot to
dig *another* hole, or perhaps twenty more
holes.

JiJi silently watches his buddy, knowing that
sometimes, it's best to observe and not say
anything at all.

Pay attention to today and remember th

ood things that happened yesterday!

Today Mode!!!

Morning sunlight sparkles over Turtle Beach, as sea turtles gather in the ocean for their daily breakfast buffet. Near the shoreline, MoCo eats sea grass while JiJi sits atop her shell. From a distance, all that is visible is the hermit crab's face peeking out from under his aluminum can. The ocean is calm, and on this morning, many sea creatures share the beach.

Out of the corner of her eye, MoCo notices unusual ripples in the water, slight movements that prompt her to stop eating. Curious, she enters the ocean with JiJi on her back for a closer look.

MoCo shrieks with excitement. Rainbows! Magnificent reds, oranges, and purples appear in a school of rainbow-colored fish! It's the dance party that MoCo played with next to Uku's home few days ago. MoCo giggles as the fish dart in shallow water, floating around her and JiJi as if to say, "Hello again!"

The fish start to head northwest, where Turtle Beach meets long strips of white sand. "Let's follow them!" JiJi says, and MoCo excitedly paddles after her fish friends. The group swims past drifting seaweed and a tiny pink rubber slipper floating by itself. A lone eel slithers nearby and dives behind a coral bed.

Overhead, feathery clouds cast shadows in the water. And there is a slight breeze.

MoCo chases her fish friends, eager to share with them her newfound wisdom and the Secret of the Lifeline, the ancient riddle that rules the oceans. They listen attentively to MoCo's stories, wide-eyed and mouths opened in awe.

JiJi tightly hangs on to MoCo's shell, trying not to fall into the ocean. Suddenly, he spots a dark sea creature in the distance, halfway between the shore and sand. The creature's head is turned in the opposite direction, so JiJi cannot see who it is. All that is visible are two wet fins and a dark, lumpy body covered in dry sand.

"Hmm! That looks like Nuku the monk seal," he observes, adjusting his glasses and squinting his eyes.

MoCo also spots the mystery creature and motions for her fish friends to join them near the shoreline. The monk seal's lumpy body— shaped like a giant, baked croissant, is dark gray and crusted in bits of algae. Whenever a mini wave washes ashore, the mysterious sea creature splashes water onto his jelly belly to keep cool.

"Is your name Nuku?"
MoCo calls out from
the shallow water,
fish friends curiously
gathering behind her.

The creature lifts his head and slowly flips onto his belly, revealing an enormous body with a tiny round head, whiskers, deep round eyes, and a blissful smile. It belongs to a monk seal!

"Alooohaaa… Howzit going?" grins Nuku, waving his left fin.

MoCo studies the mystery monk seal, basking on the beach absorbing the warmth of the sunshine and appreciating the melody of the waves. Nuku's body slowly rises and falls, breathing deeply as if he's doing beachside yoga. A baby seabird hops on top of Nuku's back, but the monk seal doesn't flinch. His calm and welcoming demeanor mesmerizes the young sea turtle.

"That's Nuku, all right," JiJi remarks, gracefully sliding off MoCo's shell. "Seeing Nuku here inspires me to teach you the final, and most important, equation of the Lifeline. You see, Nuku, with patience and practice, embodies the very essence of Aloha – the vital key to embracing the present and attaining the goal we all strive for: Today Mode."

Immersed by the kind and peaceful vibes emanating from the majestic mammal, MoCo's eagerness to understand the equation surges. She turns to JiJi and asks, "*WHAT* exactly is Aloha, *WHY* is it important, and *HOW* does it relate to the Lifeline and Nuku?

With a light and thoughtful tone, JiJi speaks to MoCo, "My friend, embracing the spirit of Aloha means harmonizing the heart and the mind. It's about being thankful, humble, and caring. Rather than judging what we see, we begin to find the beauty and joy of the moment. When we have this mindset, we can truly enjoy the beauty of the present. Nuku, is a shining example and shows us what Aloha looks like – a kind and inclusive soul who loves and cares for everyone around him.

MoCo beams with understanding, exclaiming, "Ooooh, I get it! I used to think Aloha was simply a greeting of hello or goodbye, but now I see it represents so much more! Come to think of it, the Lifeline shows us that we say goodbye to yesterday and hello to tomorrow every single day of our lives.

Everything is falling into place, and I think I know what the final equation is! Can I give it a try on my own, JiJi?

The hermit crab nods, filled with immense pride for the young turtle. MoCo turns to the monk seal, who playfully splashes more water on his belly while attentively listening. "Nuku, it seems like you live in what's called TODAY MODE," she says.

Nuku responds with flashing a smile and a shaka, the Hawaiian sign for "right on," encouraging his new friend to continue with her presentation. The seal stares at her with genuine curiosity.

"Here, lemme show you why," MoCo explains.

Turning to the tropical fish behind her in the water, MoCo calls out, "Hey fishies! Can you help me with this?" The rainbow party eagerly swims up to her, ready to assist.

From the beach, JiJi proudly observes the unfolding scene before him.

MoCo raises her fins as if conducting an orchestra. "Fishies, please write 'TODAY equals TOMORROW minus YESTERDAY!' And please write it large enough so all the creatures at Turtle Beach can see it!"

The fish obediently line up in the water, single file, using their bodies to form the words "today," "tomorrow," and "yesterday," along with the equal and minus signs. Seabirds from above can see their rainbow-colored writing on the ocean's surface, while sea urchins and bottom feeders below can tilt their heads up to study the equation as well.

Today = Tomorrow – Yesterday

Excited, MoCo announces to every creature in the ocean and sky. "This is the math equation for TODAY MODE. It is the thought process that follows when you bring TODAY front and center of the equation.

It's a mindset that encourages us to embrace the Spirit of Aloha, freeing ourselves from worries of the past and uncertainties of the future. By immersing ourselves in the present, we honor our past, shape our future, and create a meaningful today. Today, above all else, is what counts the most!"

Nuku claps his fins, appreciative and grateful for MoCo's efforts.

Suddenly, the sea turtle has an idea. "C'mon, fishies, let's have a dance party!"

MoCo gestures for JiJi to climb onto her back to join them in the water. But the elderly hermit crab shakes his head as if to say, "Go ahead without me," and settles down next to Nuku along the shoreline to watch the dancing celebration.

As though summoned by the joyful atmosphere, hundreds of sea creatures emerge from the ocean to join the impromptu community dance party at Turtle Beach. Birds flap their wings and circle above the water, while even the palm trees sway to the beat.

It's as if music plays on this world-famous beach—and only nature hears the melodies.

With her renewed energy and a deep sense of gratitude for Today Mode, MoCo gazes towards the sky and shouts, "Hey birds… *What Day Are You?*"

Aloha

ACKNOWLEDGMENT

MAHALO to my Lord & Creator, the GREAT "I AM" for making me who I AM Today. Thank you, Papa and Mama for raising me to search and find joy and goodness in the world no matter the circumstances; Oba in Okinawa for nurturing me with your love and encouragement when I was the little rascal of Misato village. You are the Jiji in this book; thank you, to all my teachers from grade school to college, who saw, recognized and unpacked the drive and energy within me to make each day count. And last but certainly not least, thank you Takako, my love and joy. Behind every successful man is a surprised wife. To all my friends and colleagues, YOU have all inspired me to write this book, as I see a little bit of the characters in the book in each one of us. If you ask me who, I will naturally ask you What Day Are You?

AFTERWORD

The 2011 Tohoku Earthquake and Tsunami devastated Japan, killing 18 thousand and leaving more than 450 thousand houseless. Takako and I visited Fukushima/ Sendai with cases of candies and provisions in hopes of meeting and encouraging the survivors. Sadly, we met no families, no children. Instead, we saw mountains of debris as far as our eyes could see. Amidst the mounds of debris were children's bicycles, walkers, and toys. We cried, wondering how in the world the survivors of Tohoku will find the will to live another day. It was during this trip that I dreamt about the LIFELINE. It was such a vivid dream that showed the importance of Today and the need to let go of our Yesterdays and not fret about our Tomorrows. Exactly ten year later, I came down with Covid and found myself quarantined in my room. It was during my weeklong "retreat" that I found the time to revisit my Tohoku notes to write this book. At the time of writing, I learned that suicide amongst children between 10 and 14 were rising at an alarming rate throughout the world due to social isolation and family woes spurred by the global pandemic. Suicide was now the second leading cause of death among young adolescents. This was why we chose to write to this audience using fictional characters from one of the most beautiful beaches in Hawaii. It is our hope and prayer that children and their parents will find solace, hope and inspiration to never give up. If this book can save even one life somewhere on this planet, we will forever be grateful.

About the Author

Steve Sombrero, a true islander by nature, proudly calls the scenic south shores of Oahu, Hawaii, his home. Born in Okinawa, Japan, and raised on the isle of Guam, he embraces a deep sense of gratitude for his journey of resilience and self-discovery that has led him to this very day.

Alongside managing one of Hawaii's largest and oldest real estate companies, Steve is a passionate entrepreneur who founded the Aloha Beer Company in 2010. Embodying the spirit of Aloha, he actively supports purpose-driven organizations, promoting youth education, and cross-border exchange programs. As an Eagle Scout and collector of proverbs and parables, Steve enjoys unearthing the profound meaning and joy of life.

What Day Are You? is Steve's first book.

About the Author

Candice Sombrero Ishikawa, a business and psychology graduate, channels her marketing expertise as the creative force behind her family's brewpub business, Aloha Beer Company, located in Kaka'ako, on the Hawaiian island of Oahu.

As the daughter of a serial entrepreneur, Candice passionately merges business innovation with a deep understanding of human behavior to foster a thriving workplace culture. Drawing from her personal journey with depression and body image, she is committed to destigmatizing mental health challenges through advocacy that promotes education, open-mindedness, and unwavering self-resilience.

When not immersed in her work, Candice enjoys listening to audiobooks, brainstorming ideas, and striving for a life of frivolous creativity surrounded by animal companions. She resides in Honolulu, Hawaii, with her husband Yusuke, and their beloved dog Packard and cat Luci.

Made for Kids, an imprint of Made for Success Publishing
P.O. Box 1775 Issaquah, WA 98027
www.MadeForSuccess.com

Distributed by Blackstone Publishing

First Printing

Library of Congress Cataloging-in-Publication data

Ishikawa, Candice and Sombrero, Steve
      What Day Are You?

p. cm.

LCCN: 2023948055
ISBN: 978-1-64146-857-2 *(PBCK)*
ISBN: 978-1-64146-855-8 *(eBook)*
ISBN: 978-1-64146-794-0 *(AUDIO)*

Printed in the United States of America

For further information contact Made for Success Publishing
+1425-526-6480 or email service@madeforsuccess.net